By the Riverside

The End of Innocence

Sylvester R. Caldwell

Sylvester R. Caldwell

By the Riverside

ISBN: 978-1-7346285-8-6

Printed in the United States of America

DEDICATION

This is dedicated to my mother, Evelyn (Babydoll) Caldwell Cunningham, and my entire family. My Grandmother, Malana Caldwell Brown, who was once the center of our family before she passed. I would like to also give a special thanks to Angelo and Mary Trimble, who kept me encouraged and pushed me to publish this work. There are so many people that in some special way have made this possible. To my children that I used to read these stories to when it was a mere manuscript, I love you all, and I pray I make you proud

BIOGRAPHY

Sylvester R. Caldwell, MS, Amridge University, is a native of Montgomery Alabama. His mother Evelyn and his two sisters, Regina, and Toni, and younger brother Dedrick, lived in Riverside Heights before moving to, the Southside of Montgomery. He fills this fiction, non-fiction book with lots of markers, and historic facts related to that part of Montgomery. His motto is. "Always remember where you came from". He looks forward to hearing from you about this piece, please reach out to him on Facebook, or email Swell278@gmail.com.

INTRODUCTION

In the late '70s, early '80s in a place called Riverside Heights. Riverside Heights was situated next to Maxwell Air Force Base and backed up to the Alabama River. This is where this story; "By the Riverside", was born. This place was considered project housing, and many families lived there. Sometimes one's youth make you unaware of your true surroundings. The stories that you're about to read could have taken place anywhere and at any time, but I am taking you along on the adventures of R.C. Cole. What are the ups and downs of life if you can't have some adventure and learn some of life's lessons? This is a story about family and friends and what it takes to live amid your heartbreak and struggle.

CHAPTER ONE

My mother once told me I could do anything I wanted if I put my mind to it. Those words would be tested for me time and time again. You see, coming from and living in the housing project for most of my young life, I did not see the meaning in those words at first. Frankly, I thought my family and those families that lived in the same condition as we did, wanted to be where they were and were happy doing so. Listening to Frank Davis next door beat his girlfriend or whoever he was going with at the time or watching grown men gamble their rent away in a dice game seemed like every day normal life.

I didn't think a dice game ended without someone being shot or stabbed over a dime or a dollar. I can recall that most men on Friday, some on Thursday, would start getting liquored up and ready for the weekend. To some, it didn't matter if they had a wife and children at home. They were going to party it up, and the saying was, "I'll be home when I get home." As I said, everyday life, and this was not unusual.

Back to my mother, I suppose she was like every other mother, caught up in her situation, having five children with no man around to help bear some of her burdens. I guess that's why every night when I saw her on her knees praying, she would have tears running down her cheeks. It seemed like whenever we were heading to school, she was walking to work. To me, my mother was everything because she did everything. She didn't talk a lot, and most often, her face had a stern, determined look on it. She was a beautiful woman, but sometimes it was hard to tell when fussing at us for what we hadn't done like homework for me and cleaning up for my sisters; my younger brother could do no wrong.

Now let me tell you when Sunday rolled around it was time for church. That rubber band that held her hair would come off, those same old uniform clothes would be replaced by what we used to call a church dress, and those run-over-the-back shoes would be replaced with a pair of heels. I guess those long walks back and forth to work wasn't all too bad. Now, don't get me wrong, some Saturday nights she would get geared up and leave us at the mercy of my older sister to go to one of the local hotspots, but eventually, as that got old to her and we got older, it was mostly a Sunday thing.

She would make us put on our best clothes and go to church on Sundays, where we would either sleep or sneak out and buy some candy with our church money. Sometimes I would listen and try to predict the exact time Sister Johnson was going to jump up and start hollering and falling out. Oh, the ladies that were near me would say in a whispering voice, "Now she knows she needs to sit down somewhere." It seems like it was just yesterday I heard Dickens say, "It was the best of times and the worst of times." Every time it seemed, it would get better for my mother, it would get worse. For every moment that was filled with a reason to cry at our situation, she tried to hold on to hope and smile—the strength of a black woman. It leads me back to what she told me, "You can do anything if you set your mind to it."

Though I'm older now, I can look back and see myself as I was then, a quiet little boy who used to watch everything around him and wonder why did this happen and why did that happen? Why don't I have a father? Why does Frank Davis beat his girlfriend? Where does the rain fall from the sky, and does God really answer prayers? You'd think I did too much thinking back in those days. I think most of my friends thought I was a little strange because I remember being outside of one of my friend's houses when I was about eleven years old standing in the rainstorm, looking up in the sky, wondering where did the rain come from. This was long before I learned it in school, but I think it was more of a spiritual thing than a scientific question.

Maybe I was a typical little black child growing up in the hood that wanted to dream beyond my circumstances. I was shy because, for some reason, I used to feel like I was out of place. My mother's older sister's friends used to say I was cute and if I was older, but I didn't see it when I looked in the mirror. All I saw was a knotty-headed, lanky little boy with a pointed nose like a white person—at least that's how my sister described me.

By the way, I'm R.C., or Rivers Cole is what my mother named me. The rest of my family would be Chantal and Yolanda Gibbs, and then Nikki and Thomas Cole. My oldest sisters had a different dad, and I guess my mother decided to give them his last name; she may have thought she was going to marry him. She didn't make that mistake with our dad and just gave us her last name. Let me tell you, having the name Rivers was like walking around with a "kick me in the butt" sign on your back, especially when I was younger. That's kind of why I adopted the nickname R.C., but later I would feel different about the little name thing.

My mother did tell me that my name had lots of meaning and roots, but back then, I was thinking "whatever." Of course, I couldn't say that out loud. You learned to keep your mouth closed, especially if there was not a question directed at you or didn't call for a response. Sometimes even if it was a question that called for a response, you better still keep your mouth closed. The way things worked was everything was my fault when it came down to it. The three sisters would stick together, and I got no support from my baby brother.

Like the time my younger brother was playing in the living room, and I was sitting at a table staring at some homework. My mother was half-asleep from a long day at work. Suddenly, "pop," a firecracker went off in the house. She jumped out of her bed and came straight to me and started putting a whipping on me. I asked, "Why are you whipping me? Thomas was the one that popped the firecracker." She said, "I was the first one she got to." That's how it was around the house. For the longest time, I believed I was found in the trash, and my mother felt too sorry for me to give me to DHR, so she kept me. At least that's the story I got from the sisters.

I had some friends then that I used to go and get in trouble with or just hang around. Troy was one of the best marble players in the hood, and Lamar was my blood brother. For that fact, we cut our hands and pressed them together and declared it so. Troy had about nine sisters and brothers, so many I don't think I ever really got to know them all, and Lamar was a single child. We used to do just about everything together, including listening to Frank tell us how he used to be some kind of big-time, big-league baseball player. In fact, when Frank was drunk, which seemed like all the time, he was all-knowing and wise. Some things didn't make any sense then, but some kind of way it ended up like he said it would. Like the one time he told us, "The things you won't do for a woman, somebody else will." Come on, Frank. We were just kids. Some things Frank said would inspire me to do right or wrong. One of the reasons I never smoked is because Frank told me that I would one day. We tried to stay out of Frank's way and do our own little things.

CHAPTER TWO

We played baseball for the local Boys Club and tried as best as we could to be on the same teams. It was like that with football and basketball too. Now everybody didn't like the idea of that because it seemed we were good at our positions and wanted to win. They wanted to win too, so to keep us from winning, they had to keep us apart. Like the time we decided we would play for the same baseball team, so we signed up. I played catcher, Troy was a pitcher, and Lamar was a shortstop.

One of the other teams who needed a catcher, or shall I say they didn't like the one they had, decided to scratch my name off the team I signed up for and put my name on their team. I had no idea and only found out about it when I went to pick up my team uniform. I got a green one when I should have gotten a red one. I told the coach about it, and he told me my name was on the green team list. Mike, Ray, and Steve, who were the neighborhood bullies, were like, "Yeah, you signed up with us." I asked the coach to look at the red team's list. He did, and I said, "See, that's where I signed my name, and someone erased it." He agreed and gave me a red uniform. This made Mike and his little gang mad, and they started saying to me, "So, you too good to play with us? Yeah, you too good, huh? Well, we will see about that."

I went to practice and didn't pay them too much attention. After practice, I jumped on my bike and headed home, and when I had just about made it, guess who jumps out of the cut? Yep, Mike and his crew. Overwhelmed and surprised, I saw there was no need to run, so I took it like a man. When my beating was over, I picked up my bike and rode home. I do remember just before it all went down, I saw Frank's girlfriend standing in her doorway, and just as I was about to cry out for help, she turned and closed the door. I remember thinking, "Damn."

I think I was mad more than anything else—not at her, but at myself for not at least trying to take them on one at a time. Somehow, I think it would have come out worse for me, but I would later get my chance with each of them one on one. I thought to myself, one day. It made me also think about people that were not as strong as I was who couldn't take up for themselves. Who would take up for them? In my mind, I decided not to be a bully and to help others the best I could. I told you I used to think a lot, and that there is a lot to be thinking about at a young age living in Montgomery, Alabama, almost right after the death of Dr. King.

Summertime, don't you love summertime in the South or everywhere for that matter? Let me tell you the projects we lived in was next to a river, and there were all kinds of things to get into. Oh yeah, the railroad tracks down by the old baseball field gave us yet more trouble to get into as well. We knew all about that white kid, Bobby Joe, and some others over the years swimming and drowning in the river. However, this didn't stop us from making our visits to Look-out Bluff and jumping and diving into the waters below. You did risk the chance of being called a little sissy or punk, but I was no sissy or punk for that matter. Our mothers had already told us we could not go swimming in the river warning, "You heard what happened to that Bobby Joe?" Playing and swinging down by the river was just too hard to resist, especially when most parents worked all day.

One of the best times to go down by the river was after it was flooded. So many catfish would get stuck in the swamp mud, it made catching them easy. We would get a screen off an old door and scoop them out of the mud and toss them into an old bucket, sort of the same way we would catch crawdads. Like with everything we did, we used to have so many we would sell some to our neighbors. I used to take some to my grandmother. After all, she was the person who took me fishing and showed me how to fish. We used to have mud up to our elbows, but we didn't have a care in the world. Even now, I think about all the snakes and other creatures that lurked in the swamp and woods. I believe I have been bitten by every bug you can think of and have had poison ivy on just every part of my skin, but we just kept on going.

One day, Lamar and I decided we would swim across the river to see who could get to the other side the fastest. I just knew I was the better swimmer than he was. Plus, everyone else was standing around, pushing us up to do it. Well, my mother said I could do anything if I just put my mind to it, so there I went. The swim over was okay. The water was calm but murky and deep. I was tired, but I had some energy left. What we didn't know was we swam with the current over. Swimming back proved to be a different story. I was fine until I got about halfway back. I noticed I was trying hard to swim back to the spot I left, but I found myself drifting downstream. It seemed like the closer I got, the heavier my arms were.

The first thing to go was my strong kick that turned into a weak flutter. Then my body sunk lower from my waist down. Pretty soon, it felt like my head and arms were only above the water. I could hear them calling, saying, "Keep swimming," but I was on the verge of giving up. The sounds of their voices were in and out replaced with the ring of the water underneath. Exhausted, I thought to myself, if I drown, my mother is going to kill me. That gave me the push I needed to make it to the other side. When I finally got to land, I was so tired I could hardly lift myself out of the water, and before I knew it, a couple of guys grabbed my arms and pulled me through the mud and laid me on the grass. I looked down and saw how muddy I was, but I was glad to be alive.

When I got home, just a little before my mother did, I had to think of what to do with those muddy clothes, so I took them and put them deep down in the dirty clothes hamper. I was hoping she wouldn't find them when she did the wash. Yes, another dumb ideal. It seemed like after about two days, they had stunk so bad she went straight for them. After that beating, it took me a while before I would try to go down to the river again. As for Lamar, he didn't get dragged through the mud as I did, and then I don't think his mother would have cared a whole lot, not that she didn't care about him. His mother was hardly home, and not because she was trying to be away. I think being a single mom, she was at work all the time—she had about two jobs. Come to think about it, I remember Lamar talking about his dad, but I never saw or met him. Lamar spent all his weekends at this grandmother's house. She lived on the other side of the projects, so we still got to hang out.

The first day we met, we almost got into a fight, for what, I don't know. I think some guys were trying to pick on him and get us to fight because he was a new kid to the hood. He wasn't scary. He didn't even back down. He stood his ground with the other boys, and for that matter, with me. Somehow, he was the kind of person that had the attitude, "We can fight if you want, or we can go to my house and look at my marble collection." We ended up playing marbles and talking all day. You can say he was one of the fellows that knew how to talk to people, and that skill would keep us out of a lot of trouble. If I was missing for an extended period of time, my sisters knew to find me at Lamar's house, or we were somewhere together. I think after a while, his grandmother saw me as much as she saw him.

CHAPTER THREE

In the South, summertime wasn't just summer days; it was hot summer days, especially when the temperature readings were a hundred and something. As hot as the days were, there were also sweaty, sultry nights. I'm talking about the first thing in the morning looking out down the street, and you could see the heat rising from the pavement like steam from a hot plate, swaying and bending in the thin air. Most apartments didn't have an air conditioner, and even if you had the money to put a window unit in, you had to take precautions not to get it stolen. Most people had what they would call a box fan—two or three situated around the house just to keep the air moving. During the day, most folk who didn't have a job would sit outside on the porch or on a pre-arranged steel swing on the shady side of the apartment building. They would leave those fans running during the day and as the sun was going down, and the locust began to come, they moved them to the windows. After a while, the screens in the windows would have a circle of dust; our apartment was no exception. That's mainly what we did to try to keep the inside cool.

When we were not at the river, we would go across Bell Street and head for the Boys Club. On most days from noon to about three in the afternoon, we could swim in their twelve-foot pool. It had a gym, pool tables, ping pong tables, a baseball field, a football field, and all kinds of stuff to do inside if you had a membership card, which was about two dollars then. Before I got a membership, I used to stand outside the fence that surrounded the swimming pool and watch the other kids swimming and having a good time. They would be pointing and laughing at us because we couldn't come in. I knew not to ask my mother for the money. I knew her answer would be, "I ain't got no extra money." So, I would go to the community center and listen to puppet Bible stories before I could get a sack lunch. It was either a government program or a church program, but the end result was to sit through some film, puppet show, or some speech about one thing or another to get a sack lunch. Why couldn't they just give us the sack lunch and let us be on our way?

"See, that's why we need a membership to the Boys Club," I argued with Lamar and Troy. We had to come up with a way to get the money to buy a membership card. One of the things we decided to do was to go around and rake and sweep people's yards for about fifty cents a yard. The Housing Authority would have all these big lawnmowers ride through the hood, cutting grass and blowing trash everywhere. If paper was in the yard, it just got run over and cut into little pieces all over the yards and porches. We had some older folk and lazy ones who thought it was too hot to be coming outside to rake a yard or pick up that little trash, so we were just right for the job.

We got up early one morning after the mowers had come through, and we set to it knocking on doors and asking if people wanted their yards raked and porches swept. After the day was done and all that raking and sweeping, we made about twelve dollars, enough for us all to buy memberships to the Boys Club. The rest we used to go across Bell

Street to Mr. Neil's store. Mr. Neil was an old white man who didn't talk a whole lot, and when you did get change, he kind of threw it on the counter. He made you feel, the quicker you came in, the quicker you needed to get out. He had in his store those penny cookies, pickles, potato chips, pig feet, Now and Laters, suckers, cold drinks, and other stuff I never paid attention to. He had the things we needed to celebrate our membership cards. After that, we decided never to rake yards for only fifty cents again. That was too much work for so little pay, but we had what we needed to go swim at the club and laugh and point at the kids on the other side of the fence.

The Boys Club was where we really learned how to swim and play all different kinds of sports. It was where we would run into some of the older guys and bullies in the hood. They were all there; however, some that we had heard about weren't as bad, at least not as bad as I had heard. There were some that were mean, and you had to watch your back and be careful around. One was called Dirty Slim, Mike's older brother. Dirty Slim, would jump the fence when the lifeguards weren't looking and get into the pool where he would terrorize the younger kids in the water. He did this by holding their heads under the water until it seemed like they would just about drown. When he felt they were close to death, he would let them up.

I recall, on one occasion, after I dove into the deep end of the high dive, Dirty was at the ladder that lead out of the pool. I didn't see him at first because I went under just before I got to the ladder. When I started to get out, I felt a hand on the top of my head just as I was about to get a breath, push me back under. I struggled for my very life at first, not knowing if someone was really trying to drown me. Almost out of breath, I suddenly pushed off the ladder and back into the deep water where I could come up for air and get a look at the perpetrator. Dirty stood there, laughing as if he had seen some amazing clown show. No one around seemed to mind until Big Joe, the club director, walked up behind him and caught him in the pool without a membership. His laughter turned into panic as he couldn't escape the husky hands of Big Joe. Big Joe was someone who struck fear even in the eyes of grown men. Big Joe grabbed his neck and dragged him to the gate kicking and cussing; he threw him out and threw his wet clothes on top of the fence where he had to climb to get them.

At the end of school, just before we would get out for the summer, there was a girl that I used to like to look at. I say look at because I never did talk to her for a lack of words to say. Just about all the guys looked at her. We would try our best to sit across the room from her, hoping someday she would wear a skirt or some tight little pants. Although we couldn't see anything across the room, the thought of it kept us in a daze. We would say yeah, I saw this, and I saw that, but believe me, it was just our imagination. Her name was Shonda Williams, and we all knew that name well. Shonda had a way of smiling where you thought she was smiling at you. The teacher had the insight to make her the person to erase the boards. Whenever I had to write on the board, I made sure my writing was big and took up most of the board. There were other girls in the class, but none like Shonda Williams.

Of all the boys that were hoping Shonda would utter some small word, it was Mike that had the most conversation with her. Some kind of way Mike's mom knew her mom and they were friends. So, of course, he felt like he had the inside track, and yes, we like the inside track. Sometimes I think he would speak and talk to her just because he knew I was looking at her. When I felt like I was getting up the nerves finally to say something to her, he would strike up some crazy conversation about dogs or cats or something of the sort.

We all knew the only time you would see Shonda was at school because Mr. Big Joe Williams was not receiving any company. If you valued your life and breath, you wouldn't get one hundred feet of her house. Not just because of Big Joe, but also little Joe, their snarling German shepherd chained outside the door. Little Joe had a strong dislike of horny boys who wanted to walk by and get a look at Shonda and her fine mother, for that matter. Little Joe was the strangest dog I had ever seen, or maybe this dog found humor in his antics. He would hide behind a bush or play sleep as you got close, and all of a sudden, he would come charging like a bat out of hell hard until the length of the chain would pull him back. You felt like your life was over looking down his throat at those crowded canines. You would be paddling your bike or running so hard like your life depended on it, and you didn't stop until you were a few blocks away. That's the chance you took cruising by her house on your bike and hoping she would look out the window and smile at you.

CHAPTER FOUR

While at school, Shonda could often be seen with her girls hanging out before, during, and after school. Toward the end of the school year, I noticed she seemed to be looking at me as much as I was looking at her. One morning, before we went to class, one of her girls approached me and gave me a note and said it was from Shonda. My hands sweaty and my mouth dry, I fumbled with the paper trying to open it up and slobber over its contents. When I finally got it open, I stood there in awe of her girly handwriting and in somewhat disbelief. I had to read it a couple of times to make sure it said what it said. Troy and Lamar were looking playfully and insistent over my shoulder, trying to see what was so amazing that I stood there silent and dumbfounded. The only thing that drew my attention away from the letter was her staring at me from one hundred feet away. Her smile hit me like a beam of light. With a clownish and unsure smile, I waved back, and as soon as I did, the bell rang for class. Feeling like I had just won some great sporting event, I swaggered off to class.

I don't think I heard a word the teacher said the whole time I was there. I was too busy pulling that now wrinkled piece of paper in and out of my pocket and reading its words over and over again that said, "I think you're cute; I like you. Do you like me? Shonda." I knew I had until the fourth period to respond, so the next three periods would be a discussion on how best to respond. Troy was like, "Tell her, yeah, and that we could go together only if you hook up my friend Troy with your friend Samantha." Lamar was like, "Man, Big Joe will kill you and feed you to Little Joe." In other words, they were of no help. I had to go at this one alone. I thought I should write back or tell her when I saw her in PE. This was going to be just right. We were going to have a field trip to the skating rink the last day of school, and Shonda was going to be my girl, and everybody would know it and be jealous. What a way to end the school year and start the summer, I thought to myself. I was riding high the whole day to fourth period PE.

After we dressed out, we all had to meet at the bleachers to get forms for our parents to sign for the field trip. After that was over, and people started to head for the volleyball nets to play volleyball, I could see she was kind of hanging around for me to come and say something to her. Feeling a little brave, I eased over to where she was and waited to hear her strike up a conversation. She smiled first and leaned her head to the side and asked if I got her note. I swallowed and prepared to let out all the things I was feeling and tell her how I was in love since the first day I saw her. I would tell her how I would ride my bike by her house just to see her standing at the window and how her smile made me feel so good inside like I was the only person around. Yeah, I was going to let her have it all, but all that came out was, "Yeah!" Then she asked me what I thought and if I would want to go with her. "Yeah, you're cute," and "Yeah, let's go together," was my response. She asked was I going to skate with her when I went to the skating rink.

Just as I was about to answer, Mike, the bully walks up. He stands right between us and turns and asks me, "What you doin' talking to my girl?" I just said, "Yeah, right," and proceeded to walk around him and finish my conversation with Shonda. He turns to her as if asking for confirmation from her, "Shonda, ain't you my girl?" She takes a step back and tells him to quit playing. He grabs her by the arm and forcefully tells her to stop tripping. I step towards him and tell him to let her arm go and go about his business harassing other folks. He shoves my shoulder and says to me, "You know what happened to you last time." I looked around and said, "I see your boys ain't here to help you now." It was on before he knew it, I was on him. I think I caught him by surprise, and I got the best of him. I had him on the ground, sitting on top of him punching and talking, "Yeah, your boys ain't here now to help fight your fight." They had to pull me off him, but oh, it felt so good to whoop his butt in front of the whole class period. Of course, when they broke us apart, he was acting like he wanted some more, and if they weren't holding him, he would be big and bad. I remember looking at Shonda and smiling with my shirt all torn and clothes muddy as she had this impressed look on her face like, "That's my man," as the teachers escorted us to the office.

After a call to my parent and explaining that it wasn't my fault, he pushed me, I really kind of sat there oblivious to what was going on around me, thinking about that look on Shonda's face and smiling to myself on the inside. In the end, I was suspended for the rest of the school year, and I would not be able to go to the skating party. Once again, damn! So, summer started a little early and unfulfilling for me. I spent the last week sitting at home and wondering what was going on at school, what was Shonda doing, and who she would be skating with.

There was no one at home during school hours, but me and Frank's girlfriend. She was way younger than Frank but older than I was. When she wasn't bruised up and had black eyes, she was very pretty, and she had a body like one of those Soul Train dancers. My mother told me not to go outside, but the house was so hot I would go and sit on the porch watching the birds and the bees and wondering and thinking. I could hear the click clacker of the train off in the distance going across the tracks, and the bell ringing at the school as they would change classes. I could hear those old men a couple of blocks over, sitting on the old iron swing joking and laughing aloud. Some were waiting for a truck to come by so they could make some money loading and unloading it.

One day, while sitting there on the porch mid-morning after I slept all I could sleep, Frank's girlfriend comes out in a sundress with nothing on under and slowly walks to the car and back. At least it felt like it was very slow to me as I found myself gawking, watching the scene unfold. She stopped at the screen door and stood there for a while, looking in my direction, but not really at me. Just as she appeared, she faded away in the background as I was trying to convince myself I didn't see what I saw. The sight triggered something in me that I did not have any control of. I made a hasty retreat back into the house to collect myself before anyone could see me. That image would appear in my dreams just about all summer long, awakening feelings I had not yet felt. The rest of the time alone, I started to think about Shonda a little differently. That weekend when school was over, I told Lamar about how I saw Frank's girlfriend half-naked outside.

I had a feeling this summer was going to be a little different than in the past. I was happy when that week was over, and the rest of the kids were out of school. I was running out of things to do and became increasingly bored as the days went by. Somehow one of my sisters found out about Shonda and me. Every day after school for that last week, I had to hear about how I was fighting over some girl and how would some girl want me anyway. Leave it to them to pour salt on an open wound and try to find out about any activity that involved a girl and me. This is one of the reasons I spent as much time away from them in the first place. Despite all of that, the one thing that kept me happy was the wrinkled piece of paper I kept from Shonda.

CHAPTER FIVE

Now that school was over, and we were deep into the summer, having that one-year membership to the Boys Club would pay off. Since I really hadn't seen Shonda or talked to her since before the last week of school, I could find out what she was up to through Big Joe, her dad. I would have Lamar ask about her every now and then. I did find out that she was spending a lot of time at her grandmother's house on the other side of town, and when she was at home, she would hang out at the Nellie Burge House. Nellie Burge was almost like the Boys Club, except

44

it was for girls. They didn't have a swimming pool so every now and then Big Joe would kick us out so that the girls could go swimming; he wouldn't even let us stand around the gate and gawk at them.

During those non-swimming days, we would go to a little place called the Sand Bottom. It was a place where underground springs had come up, and the water was clear and cool, with sand on the bottom like a beach. It was in the oddest place under a bridge not far from a railroad track. You had to know someone to find it or had been there before because it was a secret place among us. It was a long walk on the tracks unless the train would come along, and we jumped the train and rode it there. Most of the time, we enjoyed walking and picking plums and blackberries along the way as they grew wild. Most of the time, we would carry bags to put our abundant supply of berries and plums in.

That way, I could bring what was leftover home and give my mother some to sell while she was at work and some to my grandmother. My grandmother would make plum wine and blackberry cobbler just for me (not the wine). So, the trips to the Sand Bottom was well worth it. However, the tracks could be a dangerous place.

It was said that a girl was trying to jump the train and ended up losing her leg. We often thought this was another one of those stories to keep us from going down the tracks. We had been up and down those tracks so often we knew it like the back of our hands. We knew not to go to the tracks alone, so when we were at the tracks, it was in small groups, and usually, I was with Troy and Lamar or vice versa. Hobos used to ride the trains from one city to another, and some were men you didn't want to hang around or run into. We figured most of them were running from the law, homeless, or just dangerous drifters. Whenever one got angry at us or would chase us, we would take those big gray gravel rocks and throw at them; Troy being a pitcher, would hardly miss. Sometimes we would throw rocks at them just because most of them were dirty and smelly white men, and we figured they deserved it some kind of way. We just didn't know any better then.

One morning, when the girls came down to swim and Big Joe was out and his assistant was overseeing the pool, I talked Shonda into sneaking out and taking a walk with me. Of course, Lamar and Troy were with us, joking and talking about each other's mama. We went down by the tracks. This was the closest I had been to Shonda since we were in school. It felt so good to see her finally and to hold her hand. We found an empty boxcar and climbed into it while Troy and Lamar stood outside now deep into their daddy jokes. I was so nervous, and I could tell she was too. We really didn't have a lot of time before she had to go back, so I leaned in and closed my eyes and kissed her and she kissed me back. I pulled her close to me, and the kiss got longer. My hands went around her waist and drifted down to her butt. Her hands went around my shoulders. I knew there was something that was supposed to come after this, I just didn't know what, and she didn't either. So, we stood there as long as we could locked in a tight embrace.

I heard some snickering and chuckling, so I cracked my eyes and saw Lamar and Troy peeking around the corner. She pulled away, a bit embarrassed, and said she had to get back before the girls left the pool. We jumped out of the boxcar, and all made a mad dash to get back. We got back just before the girls were about to get out and leave, but she hadn't gone unnoticed. I read the lifeguard lips saying, "I'm going to tell your dad." I started feeling bad that I got her in trouble, and there was no telling what Big Joe would do. I stood there for a minute and watched as they loaded the bus. She didn't look at me, but I could see that she had a scared look on her face, and her eyes were watery.

Being around the boys, I tried not to show too much emotion; in other words, I tried to act all hard. I didn't feel like being around a lot of people, so I talked the guys into walking the tracks to Sand Bottom and picking some plums. Along the way, we listened to Troy as he would come up with one joke after another. Troy was like the class clown; he always found something funny in whatever was going on. He didn't let the fact that I was already feeling guilty for getting Shonda in trouble, he just kept the jokes rolling about how awkward I looked with my eyes closed, kissing and grabbing her butt. He made it sound so crazy that I had to laugh at myself. No matter how bad you felt, you could count on Troy to make you feel like laughing.

As we listened to Troy and laughed out loud, we picked plums. When we got closer to Sand Bottom, we heard a noise, so we crept up in some bushes to see what was going on. We thought some other kids might have found our little spot, so we were going to try to scare them off by throwing rocks from behind the bushes. It was hard to see from where we were, but it looked like it was Dirty Slim and some girl. It looked like they were doing more than standing close to each other, so we tried to get closer and get a better look. Lamar stayed back while Troy and I inched closer to the scene. As we got closer, I could see the girl was Frank's girlfriend.

In our surprise, we made a noise, and Dirty looked around to see if someone was there. We dropped everything and ran back to the tracks and didn't stop until we were well out of range. We stopped just for a minute to catch our breath and look back and started back running again. When we made it back to the Boys Club, Lamar was like, "What happened?" We told him we had seen Dirty Slim and Frank's girlfriend in the bushes doing something nasty. Lamar was like, "We got to go tell Frank." Troy and I agreed not to and told Lamar that he shouldn't either for fear that Frank would kill the poor girl. We hung around the Boys Club late into the day until just before dark and headed home.

After we crossed Bell Street, we broke off and went our separate ways. As I was approaching my block, I saw police cars everywhere. I saw one police car pulling off with Frank in the back seat. I got into the house and asked my oldest sister Chantal what was going on. She told me that Frank's girlfriend was in the hospital and that she had been beaten and raped. The police picked up drunk Frank because they knew he beat the girl. I felt a cold chill come up my back and a certain nervousness. My stomach was knotted up, and I broke out into a sweat. My sister looked at me like what's wrong with you. The conflict had set in as I pondered with my words and thoughts of what should I say? Or what should I do? I just wanted to go to bed. I think I went to bed that night the earliest I had ever gone. As I lay there listening to the box fan in the window and looking at the cracked paint on the window seal, I thought about what my mother used to tell us, "Don't talk to the police, and stay out of grown folks' business." I eventually drifted off to sleep, not looking forward to tomorrow.

The next morning, I couldn't wait to meet up with Lamar and Troy and tell them what happened, but they had already heard. We all thought it was messed up, but what could we do? We were just some kids. Besides, the preacher said everything that goes around would come around, and the good Lord would take care of it. After a couple of weeks had gone by, before Frank was out of jail, some of his buddies went to the police station and told them he could not have done it. He was with them, and a lot of people saw him at the pool hall. Frank's girlfriend was still in the hospital, and we heard that while she was in there, she had a nervous breakdown and the police couldn't get the information they needed to find out what happened to her. When we saw Frank around, he didn't look the same. Somehow, he looked older, and his clothes weren't as neat as they used to be. Instead of looking like just a drunk, he looked like a dirty drunk. The thing was he wasn't as drunk as he used to be. He didn't talk to us as much and give us that street wisdom like he used to do either. He had a sad, lonely look on his face and most of his time was spent going back and forth to the hospital, visiting his girlfriend. Frank used to tell us you don't miss what you have until it's gone.

CHAPTER SIX

We didn't go back to the track after that, and we were banned from the river, so we spent most of our days down by the old oak tree playing marbles. My sisters would be on the cement square playing hopscotch and jumping rope with some other girls. Pretty soon as the days went by, more kids started showing up, and we would play everything from dodgeball to 1-2-3 red light, and kickball. When some of the younger kids would leave, we would play hide-and-seek. This was the first time I actually had fun with my sisters. My oldest sister would come out sometimes but mostly spent her time talking on the phone to some boy. We remembered this place we use to pass by down close to the tracks that had a huge hill of sawdust—two hills, in fact. We named the place, Sawdust Mountain, and took some of the kids and headed there. It turned out to be so much fun that we would lose track of time. The objective became to get to the top and run down one side and run up the other. Many tried, only to end up face-first into the smaller side of the hill. Looking at each other with a face full of sawdust was like looking at someone with a pie in their face. We laughed so hard that it seemed to wash all our troubles away.

Back to Chantal, she was getting to the point where she didn't spend as much time with Yolanda and Nikki. She often said she felt like she was our mother because she had to watch us and do most of the cooking and cleaning. I used to hear my mother tell her she was getting to the point where she thought she was grown, but she wasn't too grown to get her butt whipped. While my mother was at work, boys would show up at the house trying to convince Chantal to let them in, but she knew as long as Yolanda and Nikki were there that wasn't going to happen. The first thing they would do when my mother got home was tell any and everything. Since school was over, Chantal was spending more time away from home, going to dances, and hanging out with friends from school. My mother wasn't having it, and they would argue about how Chantal felt like she didn't get to do anything but stay home watching us. Yolanda and Nikki would feel bad because they would say Chantal didn't like them anymore and didn't want them around her. I thought it was all girl stuff. As long as the attention wasn't on me, I was okay.

It had been a couple of weeks since all that went down at the tracks, and everybody was spending time at the big oak tree. Chantal had been asking my mother about going to a party with her girlfriends. My mother had told her yes before, but now after the situation with Frank's girlfriend, she was like, "No, oh no!" Once again, my sister was having a fit about it, but my mother wasn't changing her mind. So, later that night, when my mother went to bed, Chantal snuck out of the house. I was usually aware of all the goings-on in the house, but I didn't even hear her leave. The next morning my mother was looking for her to help make some breakfast and discovered she wasn't in her bed or in the house. She grumbled and fussed about how she was going to kill her when she got home and made Yolanda take up her slack. She left instructions for us to tell Chantal not to go anywhere when she got home.

This was going to be a free day with Chantal not at home to tell us what to do. During the course of the day, Yolanda and Nikki cooked a rubber cake; they were not trying to cook one, but that's how it came out. We ran through the house having water fights and all kinds of carrying on. We managed to get the house clean and in order just before my mother got home. However, we started to realize the day had gone by, and Chantal wasn't home yet. My sisters, having realized she wasn't going to get there before my mother got home, started to worry and, just like females, cry. When my mother got home, she asked if Chantal was home or had been home. I spoke up and told her we hadn't seen her, and she hadn't called. At that point, even I knew this was not like Chantal. She would talk about how she was going to leave, and we were going to miss her if she did, but she never did it.

My mother got on the phone and made some phone calls to her friends, asking if they had heard from her, and none of them did. In a firm voice, she told Yolanda and Nikki to hush that crying and go look for their sister. They went looking one way, and I went to the other. I went and got Troy and Lamar to help me look around. We went just about everywhere in the projects looking and asking. One or two of her friends said they saw her at the party that night. We met up with my sisters, and they said one of Chantal's friend's mother said she wasn't home either, and they were looking for her.

It was getting dark, so we went back to the house. When we got there, we told my mother we didn't find Chantal, and her friend from school was missing too. We told her that some folks had seen them at the party but did not see them leave. As I looked in my mother's face, she looked tired, and her legs looked like they were about to give out. She slowly made her way to the kitchen chair to sit down and asked me to bring her the phone. She told my sisters to go and give my brother a bath and get ready for bed. After they had gone, she grabbed my hand and told me to go and find my sister. She had a desperate look in her eye, and her voice had gone from firm to a soft, shaky whisper. I asked Troy and Lamar if they could come with me, and they quickly said, "Yeah," and we headed out the door. Before I got all the way out the door, I heard my mother calling the police.

We went out into the summer night trying to find my sister or someone who would know where she was. We hardly knew where to go or who to ask. So, we decided to go across the tracks to where the party took place. Across the track, people lived in houses, not apartments, and most of them had cars. It was a long walk, and we were mostly silent, having never been on the tracks at night, it was scary. However, thinking of that look on my mother's face before I left home, I couldn't be scared even if I wanted to be. So, we pushed on and finally made it to the house. I knocked on the door, not knowing who to ask for or what to say. I just waited for someone to answer. A dude about my sister's age came to the door and was like, "Yeah, what's up?" I asked him if he knew Chantal Gibbs and if he had seen her at the party at his house. He stepped out on the porch and said in a low voice, not to talk so loud. He said he knew Chantal and she was at the party, but he didn't see her when she left. I asked if he saw her with anybody, and he told me he saw her "with that girl she be with at school," and that was all he remembered. In the background, I heard his mother ask who was at the door, and he yelled back, "Nobody."

Disappointed, I turned to leave, and as I was going down the steps, he told us, "Hey, I saw her with Marcus." I thought *Marcus* and said, "Marcus, who?" He said, "We call him Slim." Troy and I looked at each other and said almost at the same time, "Dirty Slim." We took off running all the way back home to tell what we knew. As I ran, I thought of Frank's girlfriend and what happened to her. The more I thought of it, the faster I ran. Lamar and Troy could hardly keep up, as I dashed across the tracks and down Bell Street. When we got to the house, there was a tall, white police officer talking to my mother who was crying. We broke in and told the officer where we had gone and what we were told. We were talking so fast and all at once halfway out of breath that he couldn't understand. He told us to slow down and talk one at a time. We did, and I told him again. I even told him about how we saw Dirty Slim on the tracks with Frank's girlfriends some weeks ago. He looked at us over his glasses and was like, "Uh hum. Okay," and he would write some stuff down on a pad.

He looked at us hard for a minute and said to us, "You boys go on now and let me talk to your mother." I went to the kitchen and sat down. Troy and Lamar said they had to go home, and they did. While I was sitting there, I heard the police officer tell my mother that as for Frank, they believed they got their man. He said he would check out the thing about the party and get back to her. He told her, "Not to worry, she probably just ran away for a little while, and she may be back. It happens all the time." As he was leaving, he said, "Give her twenty-four hours and if you don't hear from her, call back."

Now, not only was my mother distressed, but she was angry as well. She told me to take a bath and go to bed she had some more phone calls to make. That night I lay in the bed, and I don't think I slept a wink. I got up late in the night to go to the bathroom, and as I passed my mother's room, I saw her kneeling beside her bed, praying with a napkin in her hand, and tears running down her face. The next morning after getting little sleep, I got up early. Troy and Lamar were also up and came to my house. My mother wasn't going to work, plus she had been crying all night long. Lamar asked, "What did the policeman say?" and I told him, "He acted like it wasn't a big deal." We decided to go to the tracks and look for my sister.

CHAPTER SEVEN

Just as we were about to go, we saw Frank. He asked me what was going on with my sister; I guess he had already heard something. I told him about the party, how she didn't come home, and how someone saw her with Dirty Slim. We also told him how we saw Dirty on the tracks with his girlfriend when all that stuff went down with her. He kind of stood there for a minute with a crazy look in his eyes. Troy added that we were about to go to the tracks where we last saw Dirty to look for my sister. He asked us to wait for a second, and he turned and walked to his house. He didn't take long to come out with a polished wooden bat that looked like it had some names of people signed on it. He came up to us and said with a low, angry voice, "Let's go get his ass!"

We headed for the tracks, not knowing what we would find or what to expect, but we were ready to get to where we were going. It seemed like we made it to the tracks just in time; there was a train coming, and it was running by the Sand Bottom. Frank didn't have any trouble at all jumping the train. In fact, it looked like he had done it a time or two. We climbed from one side of the boxcar to the other to prepare ourselves to jump off. The ride was way shorter than the walk, but for some reason, it seemed like it took just as long. My heart was racing as we approached our jump. We all made the jump okay and huddled by the bridge where Frank said he would go and look from one side, and we were to go on the other. He took off through the brush to make his way to the other side, and we crept through the wiry trees and tall grass that hid the clear water pond, the Sand Bottom.

As we approached a clear spot, I could see what appeared to be two people sitting against a tree. It scared me at first, so I ducked back into the brush and moved to get a closer look. We went around a little bit to get a better look, peeking to get a closer look at the tree. Lamar, who must have had a better view than I did, said it was my sister and her friend tied up to the tree. I didn't even look around after I heard that, I jumped from behind the bushes and ran to the tree and it was her. They were sitting there crying and shaking their heads. I tugged at the rope to loosen it, and eventually, Troy got the rope to come loose. Lamar freed the other girl, and I released the gag she had around her mouth.

Both were screaming, "Hurry! Hurry! Let's go, let's go!" No sooner than they had said that we turned and saw Dirty Slim come crashing out of the bushes with a gun in his hand. He caught Troy by the arm and put the gun to his side and yelled at us, "Ain't nobody going no damn where." Before he could finish another word, I saw a flash of light shining off Frank's bat coming out of nowhere and striking Dirty across the side of his head. He didn't even know what hit him as he fell to the ground ripping the sleeve off of Troy's shirt. Frank asked the girls if they were okay, and they shrugged their heads, "Yes." He took an eye inventory of Troy to see if he was okay, then pointed his bat as to say let's go.

We turned to leave. The girls were shaken, but okay. As we were making our way to the brush, we heard a gunshot. We all ducked to the ground and looked back to see

Dirty Slim, with all his might, aiming and firing two more times. We could see the third shot hit Frank and knocked him to one knee, but he quickly got to his feet and went over to Dirty and swung his bat. After that, Dirty didn't move another inch as blood flowed from his head. Everybody got up, ready to get out of there. I asked Frank if he was going to make it, and he said he would be alright. I looked over at Troy who was still over by the tree. I yelled out, "Come on. Let's go, Troy!" He didn't say anything. Lamar yelled out, "Come on. Let's go!" Troy just looked at us and didn't move. My sister started scratching herself uncontrollably and sobbing and saying, "No! No! No!" until she was out of breath. I looked at Troy, and the only thing I saw was a hole in front of his shirt until Frank scooped him up and turned his back to me, and I could see the blood coming from his back.

Frank told Lamar to run on ahead to the Boys Club and call an ambulance. He turned to us and said, "Come on now, let's keep it together. We got to move; we got to go." I led the girls out and down the tracks, moving as fast as we could. With Frank carrying Troy close behind us, I couldn't tell who was bleeding the worst, him or Troy, but we kept moving, and Frank kept on close behind. When we got to the Boys Club, there were police cars everywhere. Big Joe came out to meet Frank carrying Troy seeing how Frank was about to give out. The police yelled at Frank to get his hands in the air. My sisters and I were yelling at the police, "He ain't do nothing." Even Big Joe pleaded with the police not to handcuff and arrest Frank and that the man they were looking for was still down the tracks. Big Joe rushed Troy to the ambulance, and the police handcuffed Frank and made him sit on the curb. Big Joe argued with them and told them that Frank needed medical attention. They told him they had to check down the tracks first.

By this time, my mother had made it to the scene, then Lamar's mom, and Troy's mom last, looking over at us and asking where Troy was. Big Joe came over and led her to the back of the ambulance. I left my mother with my sister as she questioned her to see if she was okay and if anything happened to her. I walked behind Big Joe to where Troy was bleeding on the stretcher. His mom was shaking and crying as Troy open his eyes and said, "Momma." She cried aloud, saying, "I'm here, baby," as they loaded him up to go. I slowly backed away and turned to look for Frank and saw him still in the handcuffs, lying back on the grass looking up at the sky. For a minute, I thought maybe he was looking to the sky to see the clouds and wonder, as I did, where the rain came from, but he never looked away. He just laid there still, and in a silent moment, took one last breath.

Frank Davis, an old washed-up, drunken baseball player, who saved our lives and rescued Troy from sudden death, died in handcuffs on the curve. To me, I guess, he died a hero. Of all the men I knew in my short life at that time, he was the only one who would take time out to talk to me and my friends. That night I would pray that I would wake up, and it would all be just a dream. I would pray that God would save Troy, and we would get to listen to him tell jokes about the whole situation, and we would laugh out loud at the things he would say. In a scene that was full of commotion and chaos, people looking on and moving about, the lights of the police cars, and screams and tears, at that moment, I remember feeling all alone. I heard nothing and saw only the shadows moving about me and around me.

The police did find the body of Dirty Slim, and when it was over, they linked him to several rapes that had occurred in the past couple of years. Frank's girlfriend and some well-known baseball players and close friends, I was told, laid Frank to rest, and the police dropped all charges against him. Troy remained in the hospital for a while as the bullet caused injury to his back. We went to visit Troy in the hospital when we could, and we all would sit there just wanting things to be like they used to be. I just wanted to go home and sit in my dark room and be alone. When I finally did get home, things weren't the same. Things didn't sound the same, and things didn't feel the same. The two cars that belonged to Frank were gone. One didn't work, and there was an outline where the other car had been sitting so long with black oil that leaked from the motor.

Instead of hearing the horns and clacking of the trains crossing the tracks in the distance, I paid more attention to the angry voices of the night—gunshots and cars riding up and down the streets looking for someone to sell them some drugs. The bright colors of life now look grey and dingy, and the smell of the projects became foul to me. Before the summer was over, Big Joe moved his family out of the projects, and it would be a long time before I would see Shonda again. Things between my sister and my mother got worse. For a moment, it was just Lamar and me. We understood the moment and each other, and we had to go at it in our own ways. How I used to look at the innocence of life ended painfully; how I would see it after that would be different.   The End

Sylvester R. Caldwell